Let's Celebrate
Valentine's Day
A Book of Drawing Fun

Written and Illustrated by
Carolyn Loh

Watermill Press

It's Valentine's Day!

Introduction

It's February 14th—Valentine's Day! It's the holiday everyone loves! Valentine's Day is a time for letting others know how much you care. Your family and friends will love getting special Valentine drawings from you!

Each of the drawings in this book is shown in several simple steps. Just follow each step, adding to your drawing as you go along. Soon you'll have your own special Valentine to give to someone you love!

Remember, the best part of your drawing is what *you* add to it with a little imagination. Don't be afraid to be creative! And, most of all, have fun!

Materials

Start your drawing in pencil, so you can erase any unwanted lines. When your drawing looks the way you want it to, color it with crayons or colored markers.

paper

pencils

eraser

markers

crayons

Shapes

Most of the drawings in this book begin with these simple shapes. By softening the shapes and adding details, the drawings come to life!

 square

 rectangle

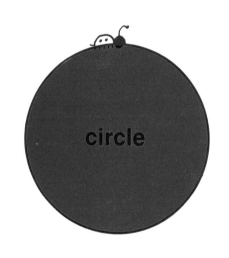 circle

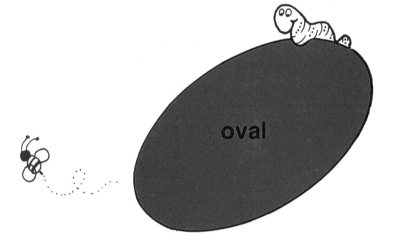 oval

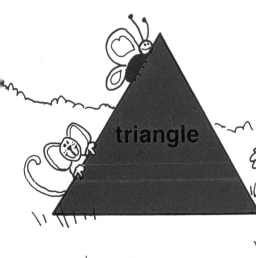 triangle

 heart

Cupid

Cupid is the god of love and a symbol of Valentine's Day. A person shot by Cupid's arrow is sure to fall in love. Don't *you* love Cupid?

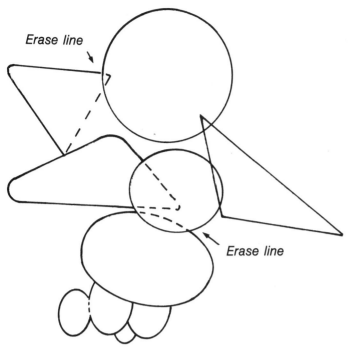

Erase line

Erase line

1. Start with circles for the head and body, and ovals for the legs and feet. Add two triangles for the wings and a triangle for the bow.

2. Add hair and shape the wings as shown. Add two little lines for the neck. Fill in the arms, hands, and clothes. Now add details to the bow.

Erase line

3. Add fingers and toes. Draw a happy face—this is Cupid's special day! Now decorate Cupid any way you like. And don't forget his arrow.

Sweets for the Sweet

There's no sweeter way to say, "I love you,"
than with a heart-shaped box of candy!

1. Start with this simple outline of the candy man: ovals form the head, hands, and feet; rectangular shapes form the rest. Add a hat on his head, a heart in his hand, and a bag of goodies in the other hand.

Erase line

Erase line

2. Fill in the details of his hat and his hair. Add two little lines for the neck. Add a string to the candy man's apron and a bow tie around his neck. Now decorate the heart-shaped box, and add fingers to grip it tightly. Add details to the goody bag too. Soften the lines of the body.

3. Give the candy man ears, curly hair, and a happy face! Then add details to his hat, shoes, and uniform. Draw a tag on the box of candy. Add more details to the goody bag— draw your favorite candy on the front. Add fingers on the candy man's hand. Now he's ready to sell you some candy!

Lovebirds

These little lovebirds sit together,
chirping from morning to night.
They sing sweet happy songs of love
to make the whole world bright.

1. Start with a circle for each head and an oval for each body.

2. Shape the feathery heads and tails. Add two triangles for each beak.

3. Add eyes, more feathers, and soften the beaks. Add the branch on which they perch. Don't forget to add the claws they use to grip the branch.

1

Erase line

Erase line

2

3

A Bouquet of Flowers

Elmo the elephant wants to tell Edna that she's his special friend. He brings her a big bouquet of roses with a note that says, "Be mine!"

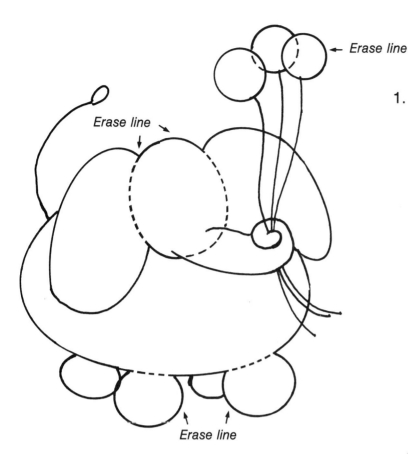

Erase line

Erase line

Erase line

1. Start with an oval for the head. Add the ears and the trunk as shown. Draw a big curved line from the middle of the left ear all the way around to the right one. That will be the elephant's body. Add the tail as shown. Add little ovals for the elephant's feet.

Now you're ready to begin the flowers. Draw three little circles attached to strings that the elephant holds in its trunk.

2. Shape the elephant's head and ears. Shape its trunk and its tail. Add its eyes, toes, tusks, and a big happy smile.

Now you're ready to shape the roses. Start with a little circle. Add semi-circles as shown. Add one semicircle for each petal you want. Then add leaves to the stems.

Erase line

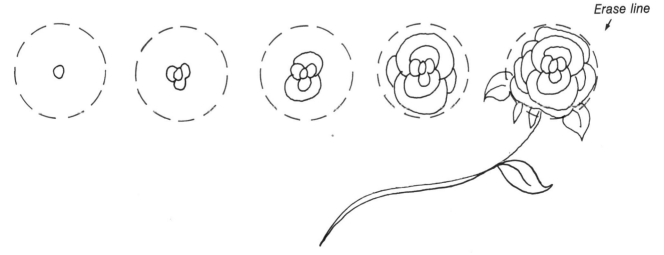

Erase line

13

Thinking of You...

The letter carrier is a busy fellow, delivering Valentines. Wouldn't it be fun to leave a Valentine for him?

1. Start with the shapes for the body, arms, and legs. Add a circle for the head. Draw the hat on top of the head as shown. Add two small ovals for feet. Draw a circle for the mail pouch with rectangular shapes as shown. Add a small circle that will be one hand; draw rectangles in the other hand. Draw the simple outline of the open mailbox and a diagonal line for the street.

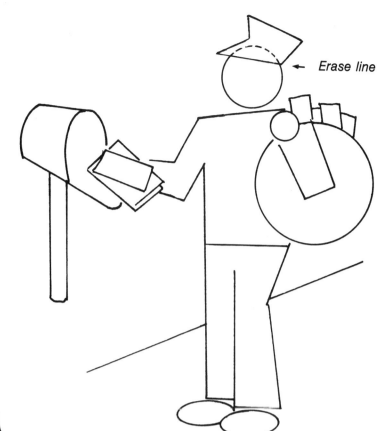

← Erase line

2. Add details to his hat and hair. Add a nose to his face. Define his arms and hands. Add details to his jacket. Don't forget to cuff the pants and give his shoe a heel! Draw the handle of the mail pouch, then add lots of letters. Put a handle on the mailbox too.

3. Add a happy face with a big mustache. Don't forget the ear! Then add a neck, a collar, and a tie. Decorate the uniform. Draw stamps on all the letters. Fill in the base of the mailbox. Replace the sidewalk with little lines that look like blades of grass. Now make the line of the mail pouch ripple to show that it's filled with letters!

The Frog Prince

How does a frog become a prince?

1. Start with a circle. Draw a wiggly line across. Draw four little legs and a lily pad, but look before you leap!

2. Shape the face. Add great big eyes and a big friendly smile. Then add spots as shown.

One Valentine kiss breaks the spell!

1. Start with these basic shapes for the prince. Add his crown, his cape, and the lily pad on which he sits.

2. Add details to his crown, cape, and robe. Add details to his shoes. Fill in his fingers, his ears, and his curly hair. Then give him a funny face!

Doubly Delicious

Share your favorite treat with your favorite friend,
and have a happy Valentine's Day!

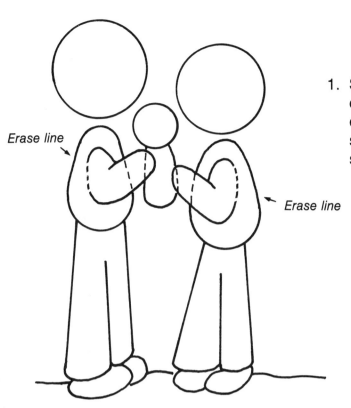

Erase line

Erase line

1. Start with a circle for each head and an oval for each body. Add the legs and ovals for the feet. Add the arms as shown. Form the ice-cream soda with a small circle and a longer oval shape.

2. Add a nose to each face. Shape the hair, neck, arms, hands, and legs as shown. Add details to the shoes. Then draw a cherry at the top of the soda and a heart at the top of the picture.

3. Add details to the hair and clothing. Add fingers to the hands. Give each child a happy face. Now, add details to the soda, including two straws for two people.

1. Start with these basic shapes to form the outline of the boy and the box.

2.

Shape the hair and the face; the arm and the hand. Put a collar on the shirt. Add details to the shoes. Draw lines on the box.

3. Now fill in the details of the shirt, pants, shoes, and box. Give the boy a happy face.

A Time for Giving...

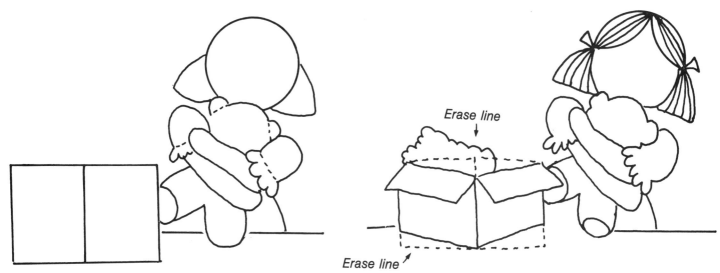

1. Start with these basic shapes to form the outline of the girl and her bear. Draw two squares to form the box.

2. Now shape the girl's hair and the sleeves on her dress. Add flaps to the box. Be sure to show the paper stuffing inside.

3. Add a happy face to the little girl and her teddy bear. Fill in the details of her hair and hands.

and Receiving

It's so nice to receive a special gift from a friend on Valentine's Day. And it's even nicer to *give* something special. Doesn't it make you feel good?

Be My Valentine!

Making your very own Valentine is fun and easy to do! Just fold a piece of paper in half. Draw your picture on the front. Then write your Valentine message inside—and send it to somebody special!

I'm Not Lion...

You're My Valentine!

I'm Not Clowning...

You're My Valentine!

1. Start your drawing with this simple outline of the lion.

2. Add eyes, freckles, and a great big smile. Fill in the nose as shown. Then shape the lion's ears, mane, and tail. Add details to the paws.

1. Start your drawing with this simple outline of the clown.

2. Add details to the hair and face. Give him a ruffled collar. Then shape his sleeves and the shoes as shown. Add fingers on either side of the heart.

3. Complete the hair and the cuffs of his pants. Fill in your clown's funny face!

1. Start your drawing of the Valentine tree with the trunk, branch, leaves, and heart. Then copy the simple outlines of the monkeys in the tree.

2. Fill in the details of each monkey's face. Add details to the saxophone. Put musical notes on either side of the monkey, and shape the leaves on the tree.

1. Start your drawing with these simple outlines.

2. Add the porcupine's funny face, paws, and prickly needles all around. Add grass and details to the heart.

1. Start with this simple outline of two frogs, a lily pad, and a heart.

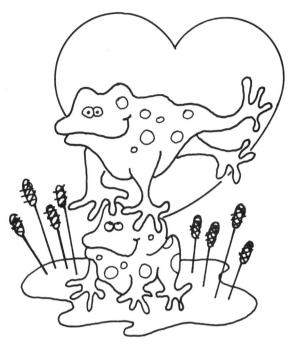

2. Add cattails to the picture. Shape the lily pad. Add details to the frogs' legs and faces. Don't forget the spots!

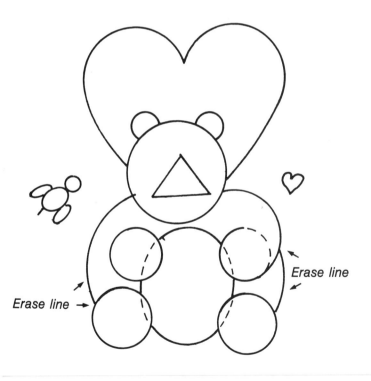

Erase line

Erase line →

1. Start your drawing with this outline of the bear, the bee, and the hearts. The oval in the middle will be the honey jar.

2. Add details to the face and paws. Shape the bear's fuzzy hair. Show honey dripping from the honey jar. Decorate the jar. Complete the bee. The broken line shows the path the bee is taking.

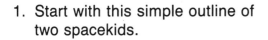

1. Start with this simple outline of two spacekids.

2. Fill in the details of the faces and bodies. Add helmets around their heads. Add the moon and stars to the sky. Don't forget the heart.

1. Start your drawing with this outline of the lion and two hearts.

2. Shape the mane and the paws, and give your lion a great big happy face!

2. Shape the head-lights, wheels, and front of the car. Shape the boy's hair and the dog's face and ears.

Erase line

1. Start with this simple outline of the boy, the dog, and the car. Don't forget to put a great big Valentine in the sky.

3. Put happy faces on the boy and his dog. Add the dog's neck and collar. Color the wheels and the dog's ears and nose. Add the steering wheel. Now you're off for some Valentine fun!

1. Start with this simple outline of the owl and two Valentine hearts.

Erase line

Erase line

2. Shape the owl's feathers. Give him a vest. Shape his wings and his claws. Add motion lines around the wings. Shade in the heart.